Ziggy and Zoey's Paw-some Adventures

Ziggy's Tail Wagging Secret (Book-1)

This book belongs to a dog lover!

_____

Written by
Pragya Tomar

Dedicated to my father

Your wisdom, your strength,
your unwavering love,
Shaped the person I've grown to be.
In every challenge I face,
every dream I pursue,
the inspiration you continue to be,
this book is for you, Papa.

ISBN 978-1-952821-21-9 (Paperback)

https://www.PenMagicBooks.com

PenMagic Books provides special discounts when
purchased in larger volumes for premiums and promotional
purposes, as well as for fundraising and educational use.
Custom editions can also be created for special purposes.
In addition, supplemental teaching material can be
provided upon request.

Table of Contents

1.

A Wish Comes True

Seven year-old Zoey sat at her carved wooden desk by the bay window in her cozy room on the second floor of a fancy old-style house in San Francisco. Her small fingers clutched a colored pencil as she sketched yet another puppy. Her room was a doggy dreamland – posters of various breeds covered the pastel blue walls, stuffed animal dogs of all sizes were piled high on her bed, and even her lamp had a playful Dalmatian base.

Outside, fog rolled over the hills of San Francisco, partially obscuring the view of the distant Golden Gate Bridge. The muffled sounds of cable cars and street musicians drifted up from below, mingling with the occasional ping of a notification from Zoey's tablet.

Zoey sighed, her hazel eyes gazing longingly at a family walking their golden retriever on the sidewalk below. The dog's tail wagged happily as it trotted along, and Zoey felt a pang of envy.

"If only I had a real dog instead of just drawings and stuffed animals," Zoey mumbled to herself, hugging her favorite plush pug. "Then I wouldn't be so lonely."

Zoey heard a gentle knock on her door. "Come in," she called, setting down her colored pencil.

Her mom, Piper, entered, holding a sleek, robotic puppy. Its metallic fur gleamed in the sunlight streaming through the window, and its LED eyes blinked in a pattern meant to be endearing.

Zoey's mom, Piper, was beautiful with long, dark hair that she always tied neatly in a bun. Her fancy glasses matched her work clothes, which made sense since she was a big boss at a computer company. Even though she was super busy making cool computer programs all day, her warm brown eyes would always sparkle with love when she looked at Zoey. Sometimes she'd be thinking about her next big project at work, but she never forgot to give Zoey a special smile.

"Look what I found, sweetie," Piper said, a hopeful smile on her face. "It's the latest model of RoboPup. It can learn tricks, play games, and even help with simple tasks around the house. What do you think?"

Zoey's face fell. She forced a polite smile, but her disappointment was evident. "It's... nice, Mom. But it's not the same as a real dog."

Piper sighed, setting the RoboPup on Zoey's desk. "I know, honey. But with our busy schedules, a real dog is just not practical right now. This could be a good compromise."

Zoey shook her head firmly. "No, thank you. I don't want a toy or a robot. I want a real, living, breathing dog. One that I can hug and play with, that will love me back."

"Zoey," Piper began, her tone gentle but firm.

"I know, I know," Zoey interrupted, her voice tinged with frustration. "A dog is a big responsibility. But I'm ready for it, Mom. I promise I'd take such good care of a real dog."

Piper looked at her daughter's determined face and sighed again. "We'll talk about it with your father later, okay? For now, why don't you at least give RoboPup a try?"

Zoey nodded reluctantly, but as soon as her mom left the room, she turned the RoboPup to face the wall. She went back to her drawing, adding even more detail to the fluffy golden retriever she'd been sketching.

"Someday," she whispered to herself, "I'll have a real dog. No matter what it takes."
Just then, her mom Piper poked her head in, a smart phone in hand.

"Zoey, sweetie, Uncle Neo will be here for dinner soon. Come help set the table."

"In a minute, Mom," Zoey nodded glumly.

Zoey's room was full of two things she loved most - dogs and cool gadgets. Dog posters covered the walls, and stuffed puppies of all sizes sat on her bed. But this wasn't just any normal kid's room! On her nightstand, a smart speaker waited to play music or answer her questions. Her special drawing tablet on the desk showed perfect pictures of the dogs she loved to draw. Even her stuffed animals were special - some had tiny screens that lit up, and others could connect to her tablet to play games with her.

The whole house was like something from the future! As Zoey walked downstairs, she passed the family's special control screen on the wall. It was like a magic window that showed all the cool things their house could do. The lights were her favorite - they would turn brighter when she walked into a room and softer when she left, like they were playing a friendly game with her. She didn't even need to flip any switches!

In the kitchen, Zoey found Mom wearing her special glasses - the ones that could show her things that weren't really there! She was talking to her computer helper about all the meetings she had that day. Their clever fridge had a screen that showed what food they needed to buy. Even the coffee maker was super smart - it knew exactly how Mom liked her coffee based on how well she had slept last night, thanks to her special watch that tracked her sleep!

Zoey peeked into Dad's office, where he was surrounded by floating screens filled with colorful computer code and 3D pictures that seemed to dance in the air! Dad owned his own company where he made amazing new gadgets. He was always busy working on his next cool invention, typing away while the glowing screens swirled around him like a high-tech light show.

"Morning, sweetheart," Ray called out, minimizing a screen with a wave of his hand. "Did you see the new VR game I uploaded to your headset? It's an interactive dog training simulator."

Zoey sighed. "Thanks, Dad, but it's not the same as a real dog."

Ray and Piper exchanged glances. They understood their daughter's desire for a pet, but their busy lives in the fast-paced world of Silicon Valley left little time for traditional pet care.

"I know it's not quite the same," Ray said, "but technology can do amazing things these days. Who knows? Maybe someday we'll have AI pets that are just like the real thing."

Earlier that week, on their way to the farmer's market, Zoey and her dad had navigated the hilly streets. Every few steps, Zoey would spot another dog – a corgi waddling down the sidewalk, a poodle peeking out of a woman's purse, a group of dogs playing in a nearby park.

Zoey's dad, Ray, was tall and fit from jogging while he worked at his special desk - it had a treadmill built right into it! His short black hair had a few gray streaks near his ears from working so hard on his company. He had the kindest eyes and was always ready with a big smile, even though he was usually looking at one of his glowing screens or gadgets. Dad loved wearing dark jeans and comfy shirts with the sleeves rolled up, perfect for when he got excited about a new idea and started drawing it on whatever he could find - napkins, notebooks, or even the kitchen whiteboard!

Zoey tugged on her dad's sleeve. "Dad, look at all the dogs! Can we please get one? Pretty please with a cherry on top?"

Ray, his attention divided between his daughter and an important email on his smartwatch, replied distractedly, "Zoey, we've talked about this. Dogs are a big responsibility, and with Mom and I so busy at work..."

Zoey's shoulders slumped. "But I'm always alone after school. A dog would keep me company!"

Ray's expression softened as he looked at his daughter's deflated face. He knelt down, meeting her eyes. "I know it's hard, sweetheart. Tell you what, why don't we look into some after-school activities? Maybe a coding class or robotics club?"

Zoey forced a smile, but inside she thought, "I don't want more classes. I want a furry friend."

Uncle Neo bounced into the dining room like a happy tornado! He was Mom's youngest brother and the most fun adult Zoey knew. His curly hair was always messy in a cool way, and he dressed like a kid who had accidentally wandered into a grown-up's closet - wearing funny computer joke t-shirts under fancy jackets. His thick glasses couldn't hide the sparkle in his eyes that meant he was up to something exciting. Uncle Neo always looked like he had the best secret ever and could barely keep from telling it!

"Hey, fam!" Uncle Neo exclaimed, giving Zoey a high-five before plopping down in a chair. "What's the latest in the world of my favorite niece?"

Zoey giggled. "I'm your only niece, Uncle Neo!"

"Details, details," Neo waved his hand, a grin spreading across his face. "So, what kind of trouble are we getting into tonight?"

Ray rolled his eyes good-naturedly at his younger brother-in-law's antics. "Neo, please. We're trying to set a good example here."

"Oh, come on, bro," Neo retorted. "All work and no play makes Jack a dull boy. Or in this case, makes Zoey a bored girl. Right, kiddo?"

Zoey nodded enthusiastically, already feeling the mood in the room lighten with her uncle's presence.

As the family ate dinner, the adults discussed the latest tech trends and startup ventures. Zoey pushed her broccoli around her plate, feeling left out of the conversation.

Uncle Neo, noticing Zoey's quietness, turned to her. "So, kiddo, your birthday's coming up. What do you want this year?"

Zoey's eyes lit up. "A dog! Please, please, please!"

Her parents exchanged worried glances.

"Honey," Ray said gently, "we've talked about this. A dog is a big responsibility."

"But I'd take care of it!" Zoey protested. "I'd feed it and walk it and, clean poop, and…—"

Piper shook her head. "It's not just that, Zoey. Dogs need training and attention. With our work schedules…"

"Yeah, I know," Zoey mumbled. "You're always busy."

An awkward silence fell over the table.

Uncle Neo, sensing the tension, smiled mysteriously. "What if I told you I know of a very special dog? One that's already trained and can mostly take care of itself?"

Zoey's head snapped up, hope blooming in her chest.

Later that evening, Zoey listened from the top of the stairs as the adults talked in the living room. The warm glow of the smart lamps cast long shadows on the wall.

She overheard their conversation. Uncle Neo said "Trust me, this dog is different. It's from a cutting-edge training program. You won't have to worry about a thing."

Ray replied skeptically, "I don't know... Remember the AI vacuum cleaner incident?"

Uncle Neo chuckled. "This is nothing like that. No rogue cleaning sprees, I promise."

"Well, Zoey would be so happy," Piper said. "And she's been very responsible lately."

Zoey held her breath, crossing her fingers so hard they turned white.

Ray sighed. "Alright, fine. But if this doesn't work out..."

"It will," assured Uncle Neo. "You'll see. This dog might surprise you in more ways than one. It's highly trained in taking care of itself with cleaning, eating, everything."

Zoey had to clamp her hand over her mouth to keep from squealing with joy. She did a silent happy dance on the stairs, nearly losing her balance in excitement.

The next morning, Zoey bounced on her bed, unable to contain her enthusiasm. Her stuffed animals flew in all directions as she jumped.

"When is he coming? What does he look like? Can we go to the pet store to buy him toys? Does he like squeaky toys or balls better? Should we get him a bowtie or a regular collar?" The questions tumbled out of Zoey's mouth in a rapid-fire stream.

Ray laughed, dodging a flying plush Chihuahua. "Whoa there, kiddo! You're more revved up than my electric car. Slow down before you short-circuit!"

Zoey giggled. "I can't help it, Dad! I'm just so excited!"

Piper entered, carrying a laundry basket. "Have you thought of a name for your new friend?"

Zoey nodded vigorously, her curls bouncing. "Ziggy! Like a funny clown dog!"

Piper raised an eyebrow. "Ziggy? Are you sure? We could go with something more... sophisticated. Like Sir Barksalot or Professor Pawsome."

"Nope!" Zoey declared. "He's Ziggy, and he's going to be the best dog ever!"

On Sunday afternoon, the doorbell rang, its chime mixing with the distant foghorn from the bay. Zoey raced down the stairs, her sock-clad feet sliding on the polished wood.

"Careful, Zoey!" her parents called after her. "Don't break any bones before you meet your new friend!" Zoey skidded to a halt at the door, her hand trembling slightly as she reached for the knob. She took a deep breath, then flung it open.

There he was – a beautiful goldendoodle with soft, curly fur the color of warm honey and intelligent eyes that seemed to sparkle with mischief. His tail wagged so furiously it looked like it might take flight at any moment. Zoey stood frozen, hardly daring to believe it. "Is... is he really mine?"

Piper nodded, smiling. "He really is, sweetie."

Zoey knelt down, gently petting the dog's head. His fur felt like the softest cloud. "Hi, Ziggy. I'm Zoey. We're going to be best friends!"

As she hugged him, Zoey could have sworn she heard a voice say, "Hello, Zoey. I've been waiting to meet you. And I must say, your stuffed animal collection is most impressive!" She looked around, confused, but her parents were just smiling at her.

Ray chuckled. "Looks like they're already communicating. Come on, let's get Ziggy settled in. I hope he likes tech gadgets as much as we do!"

As they walked inside, Ziggy looked up at Zoey and winked. Zoey blinked in surprise. Could dogs wink? And was that a smirk on his furry face? She shrugged it off, too happy to question it.

"Oh, Ziggy," Zoey said, leading him to the kitchen. "I can't wait to show you everything! My room, my toys, my secret candy stash – oops, forget I said that last part!"

Ziggy let out a bark that sounded suspiciously like a laugh.

2.

Ziggy Can Talk!

Zoey twirled around her room, her pigtails flying as she showed Ziggy every nook and cranny. The goldendoodle's tail wagged enthusiastically, his eyes following her every move.

"Look, Ziggy!" Zoey exclaimed, pointing to a wall covered in crayon drawings. "These are all the dogs I've dreamed of having. And now you're here!" She hugged him tightly.

Ziggy nuzzled Zoey, his fur tickling her face.

Zoey giggled, "Oh Ziggy, it's like you understand every word I say!"

She led Ziggy to the bay window, their noses practically pressed against the glass. The bustling San Francisco streets and the Golden Gate Bridge stretched out before them.

"See that, Ziggy? That's the Golden Gate Bridge! And look, there's the farmer's market where Dad and

I go on Saturdays. Oh! And there's Mrs. Johnson walking her pug!"

Zoey's eyes sparkled with excitement. "Now we can go on walks together too!"

Ziggy wagged his tail and let out a soft "woof."

Zoey scratched behind his ears, "We're going to be the best of friends, Ziggy. I just know it!"

"Thanks, Zoey, I'm glad to be here."

Zoey froze. "Did you just say something?

Ziggy tilted his head, his intelligent eyes fixed on Zoey.

"Yes, I can talk, Zoey. This isn't a dream. I can talk, but only you can understand me. Others will just hear barking."

Zoey's jaw dropped. She rubbed her eyes in disbelief. "But... but how is that possible?"

"I was trained by a special teacher at the school where

I came from," Ziggy explained patiently.

"Wow!" Zoey's mind was racing with questions. "I've never heard of talking dogs before! This is amazing!"

Just then, Piper poked her head into the room. "Are you talking to Ziggy? I'm sure he feels at home now.

Come on, it's lunchtime. Ziggy, we've got some special dog food for you! Uncle Neo sent his favorite dog chips."

Zoey turned to her mom excitedly, "Mom! Ziggy can talk like us!"

Piper smiled indulgently, "Oh really? That's wonderful, sweetie."

"Ziggy, say something to Mom!" Zoey urged.

Ziggy let out a cheerful "Woof! Woof!"

Zoey looked confused, "See, Mom? He said hello!"

Piper chuckled, "Oh wow! Hello to you too, Ziggy! He is a fast learner for sure. Come on honey, lunch is getting cold."

After lunch, Zoey closed her bedroom door and turned to Ziggy with her hands on her hips. "Why didn't you say anything to Mom and Dad? They think I'm making it up!"

Ziggy sat down, his tail curled around his paws. "Remember, Zoey, I told you that only you can understand me. To everyone else, I sound like a regular dog."

Zoey flopped onto her bed, her mind whirling. "So... it's like our secret superpower?"

Ziggy's mouth curved into what looked suspiciously like a smile. "Exactly! And every superhero knows the importance of keeping their powers secret."
Later that afternoon, Zoey and Ziggy strolled through the park, Zoey chattering away about her favorite spots.

"And over there is where I once saw a squirrel do a backflip!" she said, pointing to a large oak tree.

Ziggy chuckled, "I'd like to see that. Though I'm more interested in that hot dog stand. It smells delicious!"

Zoey giggled, then noticed a group of kids playing nearby. She whispered to Ziggy, "Be nice now, we need to make new friends for you."

Ziggy winked, "Don't worry, I'll be on my best behavior. Woof woof!"

As they approached the playground, a boy with a

toy robot came up to them. "Cool dog! What's his name?"

"This is Ziggy," Zoey said proudly. "He's my new best friend."

The boy grinned, "Awesome! Does he know any tricks?"

Zoey looked at Ziggy, a mischievous glint in her eye. "Oh, you have no idea..."

That night, as Zoey snuggled into bed, Ziggy curled up at her feet.

"Ziggy?" Zoey whispered.

"Yes, Zoey?"

"Can you tell me a bedtime story

Ziggy's eyes twinkled in the dim light. "How about The Tale of the Intergalactic Squirrel Chase?"

Zoey's eyes widened with excitement. "Yes, please!" As Ziggy began his fantastical story, Zoey drifted off to sleep, dreaming of the amazing adventures she and her extraordinary new friend would have.

3.

Ziggy Goes to School

Sitting on a place of honor on Zoey's bed was Valerie, her high-tech interactive doll. Unlike the other toys, Valerie was special - a cutting-edge prototype gifted to Zoey from her Uncle Neo. With her color-changing hair and the interactive touch screen embedded in her dress, Valerie was more than just a plaything.

"Good morning, Zoey!" Valerie chirped, her voice emanating from hidden speakers. "Would you like to play a game or work on your homework?"

Zoey smiled at the doll. "Not now, Valerie. But can you remind me about it later?"

"Of course!" Valerie replied, her eyes lighting up as she set a reminder. "I'll alert you after school. By the way, your math homework is due today. Don't forget to pack it!"

"Thanks, Valerie," Zoey said, grabbing her backpack. As Zoey headed downstairs, Valerie called out, "Have a great day at school!"

"Another school day," Zoey sighed, patting Ziggy's head. "I wish you could come with me, Ziggy."

Suddenly, her eyes lit up. "Wait a minute... why can't you?" Ziggy's ears perked up, a mix of curiosity and concern in his eyes.

"We have 'Show and Tell' today," Zoey explained excitedly. "I could bring you for that, and then... you could just stay for the rest of the day!"

"Zoey, I'm not sure that's a good idea," replied Ziggy.

"Oh, don't worry," Zoey giggled, mistaking Ziggy's concern for excitement. "It'll be fun! You'll see!"

At breakfast, Zoey could barely contain her excitement. "Mom, can I take Ziggy for 'Show and Tell' today?" she asked innocently.

Piper looked up from her coffee. "Sure, honey. I'll drop him off at lunchtime for you."

"No!" Zoey said quickly. "I mean... show and tell is the first thing... I can take him in my bigger backpack. He'll fit; I promise!"

Piper raised an eyebrow but shrugged. "Alright, if you're sure. Just don't let him be a distraction, okay?"

Soon, Zoey was walking to school with an unusually lumpy backpack. Every few steps, a golden furry ear or nose would poke out.

"Ssh, Ziggy!" Zoey whispered. "We're almost there!" As they approached the school, Zoey saw the principal, Mr. Stern, greeting students at the entrance. She gulped and tried to look casual as she walked past.

"Good morning, Zoey," Mr. Stern said. "My, that's a large backpack today!"

"Oh, um, lots of... books!" Zoey stammered. At that moment, Ziggy sneezed.

Mr. Stern looked puzzled. "Did your backpack just... sneeze?"

"No! That was me!" Zoey fake-sneezed quickly.

"Must be allergies. Bye, Mr. Stern!"

She hurried inside, heart pounding. That was close! In class, Zoey's teacher, Ms. Maple, began the day with 'Show and Tell'.

"Zoey, I believe you have something to share with us today?" Ms. Maple smiled.

Zoey nodded eagerly and unzipped her backpack. Out popped Ziggy, looking slightly rumpled but tail wagging.

"This is my dog, Ziggy!" Zoey announced proudly. The class oohed and aahed. Tommy, sitting in the back, gave a thumbs up.

"He's not as cool as my Buddy," Tommy teased, "but he's pretty cute!"

Mia raised her hand. "Can he do any tricks like Pixie?" She held up a small projector, which displayed a hologram of her cat Pixie doing a front flip.

Zoey gulped. She knew Ziggy could probably outsmart any dog, but that a flip needed practice.

"Um, Ziggy, sit!" she commanded. Ziggy obediently sat, then flopped over dramatically, playing dead. The class erupted in giggles. "He's funny!" someone shouted.

As the day progressed, keeping Ziggy hidden became increasingly challenging. In math class, Ms. Maple wrote a tricky problem on the board.

"Can anyone solve this?" she asked.

Ziggy, hidden under Zoey's desk, whispered the answer. Without thinking, Zoey blurted it out.

Ms. Maple looked impressed. "Why Zoey, I had no idea you were such a math whiz!"

Zoey blushed, patting Ziggy gratefully under the desk.

Lunchtime brought new challenges. Zoey snuck Ziggy into the cafeteria, hiding him under the table. But the lunch lady's cat, Mr. Whiskers, spotted Ziggy and arched his back, hissing.

Ziggy couldn't resist. He let out a playful "Woof!",

sending Mr. Whiskers scrambling across the cafeteria, knocking over trays in his wake.

Food flew everywhere. In the chaos, Zoey managed to sneak Ziggy back into her backpack.

"Who brought a dog to lunch?" the lunch lady demanded, covered in spaghetti sauce.

Zoey sank low in her seat, trying to look innocent.

P.E. class was another adventure. As the kids played soccer, Ziggy watched longingly from Zoey's open backpack by the bleachers.

Suddenly, a ball rolled right up to him. Unable to resist, Ziggy bopped it with his nose, sending it flying across the gym and scoring an unexpected goal for Zoey's team.

"Whoa, Zoey!" her teammates cheered. "How did you do that?"

"I've been... practicing?" Zoey said weakly. The real challenge came in science class. Mr. Proton was demonstrating a complex chemical reaction.

"Now, if I add just three drops of this solution..." he began.

Ziggy, fascinated, edged closer for a better look. His tail brushed against a rack of test tubes, causing a chain reaction. Liquids mixed, smoke billowed, and suddenly, a small rainbow appeared in the classroom.

The students gasped in awe. Mr. Proton looked flabbergasted.

"I've been trying to achieve this reaction for years!" he exclaimed. "How did this happen?"

All eyes turned to Zoey's desk, where Ziggy sat, tail wagging innocently.

"Zoey," Mr. Proton said slowly, "is that a dog?" The secret was out. But to Zoey's surprise, instead of being angry, Mr. Proton was thrilled.

"What a remarkable animal!" he exclaimed. "He seems to have a nose for science!"

Word spread quickly. Soon, Mr. Stern arrived, looking stern indeed.

"Young lady," he began, but then he saw Ziggy trying to solve a Rubik's cube with his paw, Mr. Stern's expression softened.

"Well, I must say, I've never seen such a well-behaved dog in school before," he mused. "Perhaps we should consider a 'Bring Your Pet to School' day..."

On the walk home, Zoey hugged Ziggy tight. "We did it, boy! Though maybe next time, we should just stick to 'Show and Tell'."

Ziggy woofed in agreement. Zoey whispered, "You know, for a moment there in science class, it almost seemed like you understood what was happening. Isn't that silly?"

Ziggy just wagged his tail in response.

4.

New Tricks for an Old Dog

Zoey trudged into the kitchen after school, her usual bounce noticeably absent. Ziggy trotted over, tilting his head in concern.

"What's wrong?" he asked.

Zoey sighed, absentmindedly scratching behind Ziggy's ears. "Nothing, Ziggy. Just... Tommy was showing everyone videos of Buddy doing all these cool tricks. And Mia's cat, Pixie, can do backflips! I guess I just felt a little... left out."

Ziggy's ears perked up. "I can always learn new tricks. Will you teach me?"

Zoey's eyes lit up. "Can you really?"
Ziggy wagged his tail enthusiastically in response.

The next day, Zoey transformed the backyard into a doggy boot camp. She'd set up an obstacle course using cardboard boxes, hula hoops, and her dad's golf clubs . A tablet propped up on a lawn chair displayed tutorial videos for various dog tricks.

"Okay, Ziggy," Zoey said, hands on hips and looking very serious. "Let's start with something easy. Roll!" Ziggy looked at her blankly, then slowly lowered himself... halfway.

"No, no," Zoey giggled. "All the way, silly!"

Ziggy completed the roll, making a show of wobbling a bit as if it were difficult.

"Good boy!" Zoey cheered, offering a treat. "Now... stay!"

As Zoey backed up, Ziggy waited precisely three seconds before bounding after her, nearly knocking her over in an enthusiastic tackle.

"Whoa!" Zoey laughed, trying to fend off Ziggy's playful licks. "I guess we need to work on that one!"

Over the next hour, Ziggy "struggled" with backflips (getting tangled in his own legs), front flips (dramatically flopping over, then immediately popping back up), and fetching (bringing back everything except the ball Zoey threw).

By the end of the session, Zoey was breathless from laughing.

"You did great, boy!" Zoey said, giving Ziggy a big hug. "We'll keep practicing, and soon you'll be the star of the dog park!"

Ziggy wagged his tail excitedly.

The following weekend, Zoey decided it was time for a public practice session. As they approached the local dog park, Ziggy could hear the excited barks and yips of his canine neighbors.

"Ziggy! Zoey!" a familiar voice called out. It was Tommy, waving enthusiastically as Buddy the golden retriever bounded towards them.

"Hi Tommy!" Zoey replied, trying to sound upbeat despite her nervousness. "We've been working on some new tricks. Want to see?"

"Sure!" Tommy grinned. "Buddy just learned to balance a treat on his nose. Show 'em, boy!"

Buddy sat obediently as Tommy placed a biscuit on his nose. For a moment, the golden retriever was the picture of concentration. Then, a butterfly fluttered by. Buddy's eyes followed it, his head tilted... and the treat fell, bouncing off his nose and into his waiting mouth.

"Well," Tommy laughed, "he's still working on the 'wait' part."

Zoey giggled, feeling a bit more relaxed. "Okay, Ziggy. Let's show them our sit-stay combo!"

Ziggy sat promptly, then fixed his eyes on Zoey as she backed up. One step... two steps... three-- Ziggy's ears suddenly perked up, and he darted off, chasing after a squirrel that had appeared at the edge of the park.

"Ziggy!" Zoey called, her cheeks flushing with embarrassment. "Come back!"

Ziggy led Zoey on a merry chase around the park,

dodging around trees and leaping over benches, always staying just out of reach.

Finally, panting and giggling, Zoey collapsed onto the grass. Ziggy trotted over, tail wagging, and dropped a stick at her feet.

"Oh, so now you want to play fetch?" Zoey laughed, reaching out to ruffle his fur.

Just then, a tabby cat trotted up, followed by Mia with wild curly hair and glasses.

"Hi! Meet Pixie, my cat!

Pixie let out a series of yawns that somehow managed to sound friendly. Her golden brown fur gleamed in the sunlight, and its eyes mimicked a friendly wink.

"Wow," Zoey breathed, eyeing Pixie with a mixture of awe and envy. "What can Pixie do?"

 Mia's eyes lit up. "Watch this! Pixie, jump!"

Pixie jumped. It did backflips, walked on its front paws.

"That's... amazing," Zoey said, trying to keep the disappointment out of her voice. She looked down at Ziggy, who was sitting quietly by her side. "We're still working on stay."

Mia smiled kindly. "Hey, every pet learns at their own pace. I'm sure Ziggy has lots of other great qualities!"

As they chatted, a commotion broke out on the other side of the park. A cat had somehow perched high up in a tree, hissing at the barking dogs below.

"Oh no!" Tommy exclaimed. "That's Mrs. Johnson's cat, Whiskers. She's terrified of heights!"

The children rushed over, but it was clear the cat was too high for anyone to reach.

Zoey looked at Ziggy, an idea forming. "Ziggy," she whispered, "I know this is a big ask, but do you think you could try to help Whiskers?"

Ziggy barked in response, then began to approach the tree. He circled it once, then twice, as if assessing the situation. Then, to everyone's amazement, he began to climb. Using the rough bark for traction, Ziggy made his way up the tree with a grace that seemed almost impossible for a dog. The gathered crowd watched in awe as he reached Whiskers' branch.

Carefully, gently, Ziggy coaxed the terrified cat onto his back. Then, with incredible balance and agility, he made his way back down the tree, leaping the last few feet to land softly on the grass.

Whiskers immediately ran to Mrs. Johnson, who had just arrived at the park. The old lady scooped up her cat, tears of relief in her eyes.

"Oh, thank you, thank you!" she cried. "What a remarkable dog!"

The park erupted in cheers and applause. Zoey stood frozen, her mouth hanging open in shock.

"Zoey!" Tommy exclaimed, running over. "That was incredible! I've never seen a dog do anything like that!"

"I... I didn't know he could do that," Zoey stammered, staring at Ziggy in wonder.

Mia joined them, her eyes wide behind her glasses. "That was even more impressive than Pixie's tricks! Your dog is amazing, Zoey!"

As the excitement died down and they headed home, Zoey's mind was racing. How had Ziggy done that? She'd been trying to teach him simple tricks, and suddenly he was rescuing cats from trees like a canine superhero!

"You know, Ziggy," she said as they walked, "I wanted to teach you tricks to impress everyone. But it turns out, you had some pretty impressive tricks of your own!" She laughed, hugging him tightly. "You really are the best dog ever."

As they reached their front door, Zoey paused. "Hey Ziggy," she said thoughtfully, "Maybe tomorrow we can work on that tree-climbing trick again. You never know when we might need to rescue another cat!" "Sounds good!" Ziggy nodded.

5.

The Midnight Intruder

The San Francisco skyline twinkled like a sea of stars against the inky night sky. In Zoey's cozy house, shadows danced on the walls as a cool breeze rustled the curtains. Zoey's parents were out at the grand Moscone Center for a tech convention, where the latest AI robot, promising to revolutionize household chores, was being unveiled.

Meanwhile, Ashley, their freckle-faced 16-year-old neighbor with fiery red hair, was in charge. She sat on the living room couch, scrolling through her phone, occasionally glancing at the TV playing a rerun of a superhero cartoon.

"Alright, kiddo," Ashley said, stretching and yawning. "It's way past your bedtime. You've had your pasta, watched your show, and now it's time for all superheroes-in-training to go to bed."

Zoey, still buzzing with energy, bounced on her toes. "But I'm not tired! Can't I stay up just a little longer? Pretty please?"

Ashley chuckled, ruffling Zoey's curly hair. "Nice try, squirt. Your parents would have my head if I let you become a night owl. Come on, up you go!"

As Zoey trudged up the creaky stairs, Ziggy followed close behind, his tail wagging.
In her room, Zoey changed into her favorite star-patterned pajamas.

As Zoey snuggled under her warm blanket, Ziggy curled up at the foot of her bed, his alert eyes scanning the room protectively.

"Goodnight, Ziggy," Zoey mumbled, already drifting off. "You're the best dog ever..."

"Night night, Zoey," replied Ziggy. The house settled into a peaceful quiet, broken only by the distant hum of traffic and the occasional hoot of an owl.

Around 10 PM, Ashley's phone buzzed insistently. She glanced at the screen, her face lighting up. It was her boyfriend, Jake.

"Hey you," she whispered, stepping onto the porch. "I can't talk, I'm babysitting."

"Just for a few minutes," Jake pleaded. "I'm right around the corner. I really need to see you."

Ashley bit her lip, conflicted. "Okay, but only for a moment," she conceded, glancing back at the quiet house.

Unknown to Ashley, a van had been idling down the street, its occupants watching the house intently. As Ashley walked to the corner, two figures dressed in black slipped out of the van and crept towards the side of the house.

Inside, Ziggy's ears perked up at a faint scratching sound. His eyes snapped open, scanning the dark room. Zoey was fast asleep, oblivious to the danger approaching.

Ziggy padded silently out of the room, his nose twitching as he caught an unfamiliar scent. He crept down the stairs, every muscle tense.

In the kitchen, a window slid open with a soft scrape. A gloved hand reached in, disabling the alarm system with a high-tech device. Two men in black slipped inside, their eyes gleaming behind ski masks.

"Rich tech executives," one whispered. "This place must be full of goodies."

Ziggy growled low in his throat, hackles rising. The intruders froze.

"I thought the house was supposed to be empty," the second man hissed.

"It's just a dog," the first replied, pulling out a treat from his pocket. "Here, nice doggy..."

But Ziggy wasn't fooled. He barked loudly, the sound echoing through the house.

Upstairs, Zoey jolted awake. "Ziggy?" she called out, fear creeping into her voice.

The intruders cursed. "Grab what you can, we need to move fast!"

Ziggy raced back upstairs, his heart pounding. He burst into Zoey's room. "Zoey! Wake up! There are bad men in the house. You need to hide in the closet and call 911 on your smart watch."

Zoey's eyes widened in terror. "But... but... I'm scared, Ziggy!"

"I know, but you need to be brave. I'll protect you, I promise. Now go!"

Trembling, Zoey slipped into her closet, burrowing behind hanging clothes. With shaky fingers, she dialed 911 on her smartwatch, its blue glow illuminating her frightened face.

"911, what's your emergency?" a calm voice answered.

"I'm Zoey," she whispered, her voice quivering. "I'm seven. There are bad men in our house. I'm so scared. Please help us!"

"You're doing great, Zoey," the dispatcher reassured her.

"We're sending help right away. Can you tell me your address?"

As Zoey gave the information, she could hear heavy footsteps on the stairs. Her heart raced, and she clasped a hand over her mouth to stifle a whimper.

Outside the closet, Ziggy stood guard, his body tense and ready. The door creaked open, and a beam of flashlight cut through the darkness.

"Check everywhere," a gruff voice commanded. "These tech types always have hidden safes."

Ziggy growled, positioning himself between the intruders and the closet. The men jumped, startled.

"It's that dog again," one hissed. "Get rid of it!"

The other man reached for Ziggy, but the dog was too quick. He darted between their legs, nipping at their heels and making them stumble.

"Argh! Catch that mutt!"

In the closet, Zoey listened to the chaos, her heart pounding. "Please hurry," she whispered to the 911 dispatcher.

Suddenly, police sirens wailed in the distance. The intruders cursed.

"We've got to get out of here!"
They turned to flee, but Ziggy was determined to stop them. He latched onto one man's pant leg, refusing to let go.

"Let go, you mangy mutt!" the man yelled, trying to shake Ziggy off.

The commotion bought precious time. Red and blue lights flashed outside, and the sound of car doors slamming echoed through the night.

"Police! Don't move!" a voice boomed from downstairs.

The intruders, realizing they were cornered, raised their hands in surrender just as the police burst into the room.

A kind-faced officer gently opened the closet door. "Zoey? It's safe now. You can come out."

Zoey emerged, tears streaming down her face. She

threw her arms around Ziggy, burying her face in his fur. "You saved me, Ziggy! You're a hero!"

As the police took statements and secured the scene, Zoey's parents rushed in, faces pale with worry.

"Oh, sweetie!" her mom cried, enveloping Zoey in a tight hug. "We were so terrified when we got the call. Are you okay?"

"Ziggy protected me," Zoey said proudly, her voice muffled against her mom's shoulder. "He's the bravest, smartest dog ever."

Her dad knelt down, patting Ziggy's head. "Good boy, Ziggy. You're a true hero."

As the excitement died down and the house settled back into quiet, Zoey snuggled with Ziggy in her bed, unable to sleep.

"Ziggy?" she whispered.

"Yes, Zoey?"

"How did you know what to do? You're so brave and smart."

Ziggy nuzzled her hand. "I just want to keep you safe, always. That's what friends are for."

As Zoey drifted off to sleep, feeling safe and loved, she couldn't help but think: Ziggy is a special dog, and he really cares for me. She knew one thing for sure — he was the best friend she could ever ask for.

6.

The Spectacular Dog Show

Zoey's pigtails bounced as she skipped through Golden Gate Park, Ziggy trotting beside her. The morning sun glinted off the dew-covered grass, and the air was filled with the sounds of chirping birds and distant barks.

"Look, Ziggy!" Zoey suddenly exclaimed, screeching to a halt in front of a community bulletin board. "The San Francisco Sensational Dog Show! It's next weekend!" Her eyes sparkled with excitement as she read the flyer aloud. "Test your dog's skills! Win amazing prizes! Be crowned the most paw-some pooch in the city!"

Ziggy tilted his head, a hint of worry in his eyes.

"I don't know, Zoey. A dog show sounds like a lot of attention. Plus, I'm not sure I'd be very good at tricks."

But Zoey was already lost in a daydream, imagining Ziggy wearing a crown and draped in a blue ribbon. "Oh, come on, Ziggy! It'll be fun! Besides, you're the smartest dog I know. We'd win for sure!"

Ziggy sighed, knowing resistance was futile. "Alright, let's do this."

Zoey grinned, giving Ziggy a big hug. "Now, let's go practice! I've got some great ideas for our routine."

Over the next week, the backyard became their training ground. Piper and Ray watched from the kitchen window, sipping their coffee and chuckling at the scene.

"Sit, Ziggy! Now roll over!" Zoey commanded, waving a treat in the air.

Ziggy flopped onto his back. "Like this?" he whispered, his legs comically flailing in the air.

Zoey giggled. "No, silly! You have to roll all the way over. Like this!" She demonstrated, rolling on the grass and coming up with leaves in her hair.

Zoey's parents watched Zoey from their bedroom on the second floor.

Ray turned to Piper, grinning. "Should we tell her that's not how dogs roll over?"

Piper shook her head, laughing. "No, let them figure it out. It's adorable."

As they practiced, Ziggy picked up on Zoey's training techniques. By the end of the week, they had a routine that was... unique.

The day of the show arrived, and the park was transformed into a canine carnival. Dogs of all shapes and sizes paraded around, some in elaborate costumes, others showing off tricks. The air buzzed with excitement, punctuated by barks and the beeping of various electronic devices used for scoring and timing.

As they registered, a perfectly groomed poodle pranced by, nose so high in the air it was a wonder she could see where she was going.

"Well, well," a snooty voice remarked. "Look, Princess. It seems they're letting just anyone enter these days."

Zoey turned to see a woman in a fancy hat, holding the poodle's leash. Before she could respond, a slobbery tongue attacked her face.

"Buddy! No!" Tommy ran up, trying to control his enthusiastic golden retriever. "I'm so sorry! He just loves making new friends", said Tommy.
Zoey laughed, wiping her face. "He is adorable. Ziggy is much less... drooly."

Suddenly, a commotion drew their attention. A sleek, metallic dog was rolling through the crowd, its owner frantically pushing buttons on a remote control.

"Beep boop! I am RoverTron 3000. Prepare to be amazed by my superior canine capabilities!" the robot dog announced in a monotone voice, its LED eyes flashing with each word.

Tommy leaned in, whispering, "That's Mr. Tech's latest invention. Rumor has it, he spent more on that robot than most people spend on a house!"

The show began with obedience trials. Princess performed flawlessly, earning a standing ovation from Mrs. Fancypants (and polite applause from everyone else). Buddy... well, Buddy tried his best, charming the crowd by sitting when told to stay, rolling over when told to shake, and attempting to befriend every squirrel in the vicinity.

When it was Ziggy's turn, he walked the line between impressive and believable. He sat, stayed and came when called, but always with a slight delay, as if he was really thinking about whether to obey or not.

During the agility course, RoverTron 3000 zipped through the obstacles at lightning speed, leaving a trail of singed grass behind. Princess got her poof caught in a tunnel and emerged looking like she'd been through a wind tunnel. Buddy joyfully knocked over half the jumps, treating the whole course like a giant game.

Ziggy completed the course gracefully, but stumbled on the last jump, earning sympathetic "awws" from the crowd.

Finally, it was time for the freestyle round. As they waited their turn, Zoey noticed Ziggy seemed nervous.

"What's wrong, boy?" she asked, scratching behind his ears.

Ziggy whined softly.

Zoey knelt down, hugging him tight. "You're amazing, Ziggy. Don't be afraid to show it! Just... maybe don't solve any algebra problems or anything, okay?"

Inspired by Zoey's words (and amused by her joke), Ziggy took center stage. He began with simple tricks, then gradually increased the complexity. He spelled out "WOOF" with letter blocks (carefully misspelling it as "WOFO" instead of "WOOF"), played a Simon game with his paw (after pretending to chew on it for a while), and even played "Mary Had a Little Lamb" on a tiny piano (with a few deliberate wrong notes).

The crowd was awestruck. Buddy watched with admiration, his tail wagging so hard his whole body shook. Princess sniffed disdainfully, while Mrs. Fancypants muttered something about "circus tricks."

As Ziggy took a bow, Princess slinked towards him, paw outstretched as if to congratulate him. But at the last moment, she swiped at his legs.

Ziggy jumped to avoid the trip, but he bumped into RoverTron 3000. The robot dog's eyes began to flash red.

"Error! Error!" it beeped loudly. "Initiating Chaos Mode!"

RoverTron started spinning wildly, shooting tennis balls from a hidden compartment. Dogs barked, people screamed, and the show descended into chaos. Mr. Tech frantically pushed buttons on his remote, but nothing worked.

"Ziggy, we have to do something!" Zoey cried, ducking to avoid a flying tennis ball.

Ziggy barked in agreement, quickly formulating a plan. He ran to Buddy, barking and gesturing with his head. Somehow, the goofy golden retriever seemed to understand. Together, they started herding the panicked crowd to safety.

To everyone's surprise, Princess joined in, using her agility to round up the smaller dogs. Mrs. Fancypants watched in shock as her prissy poodle got her paws dirty for the first time.

Meanwhile, Ziggy approached RoverTron, dodging the tennis ball barrage. With a carefully calculated leap, he landed on RoverTron's back. Using his paw, he pressed a sequence of buttons that looked random but was actually a complex shutdown code.

The robot dog powered down, and the chaos subsided. The park fell silent, then erupted into cheers.

As the dust settled, the judges huddled in discussion. Finally, they approached the center ring.

"In light of today's extraordinary events," the head judge announced, "we've decided to present our awards a bit differently. The blue ribbon for Best in Show goes to... Buddy!"

Tommy's jaw dropped as Buddy pranced forward, proudly accepted his ribbon and promptly tried to eat it.

"For his remarkable skills and quick thinking, we present Ziggy with our special 'Hero of the Day' award!"

Zoey hugged Ziggy tightly as he was given a shiny gold medal. Even Princess and Mrs. Fancypants seemed impressed, offering congratulatory nods.

That evening, as Zoey and Ziggy cuddled in bed, Zoey couldn't stop talking about the day's events.
"You were amazing, Ziggy! The way you played the piano, and then saved everyone from that crazy robot dog! You're like... a super-dog or something!"
Ziggy wagged his tail, and said "Thank you, Zoey!"

"You know what?" Zoey yawned, snuggling deeper under her covers. "Winning that special award was even better than Best in Show. You're a real hero, Ziggy."
Zoey drifted off to sleep with Ziggy watching over her.

7.

Ziggy's Surprise Party Pandemonium

Zoey sat bolt upright in bed, her eyes wide. "Ziggy!" she exclaimed, startling the goldendoodle sleeping at her feet. "When's your birthday?"

Ziggy blinked sleepily. "My what?"

"Your birthday! Oh no, we've never celebrated it!" Zoey's face fell, but then brightened with determination. "That's it. We're throwing you a surprise party!"

"I guess I can pretend to be surprised!" quipped Ziggy.

Over breakfast, Zoey shared her plan with her parents. Piper and Ray exchanged amused glances.
"Honey," Piper began gently, "Do dogs even have birthday parties?"

"Well, this one will!" Zoey declared, pointing her spoon at Ziggy, who was pretending to be very interested in his kibble.

Ray chuckled. "Alright, party planner. What do you need?"

For the next week, Zoey was a whirlwind of secret preparations. She whispered with her parents, hastily hid party supplies whenever Ziggy entered a room, and made mysterious phone calls to her friends.

Ziggy, for his part, played along, pretending not to notice Zoey's poorly concealed "Operation Birthday Surprise" notebook or the dog-shaped cake pan hidden behind the cereal boxes.

The day before the party, Zoey attempted to bake a dog-friendly cake. The kitchen soon looked like a flour bomb had exploded.

"No, Ziggy!" Zoey giggled, shooing him away. "You can't see your cake yet!"

That evening, Ray suggested using a new invitation app to send out evites. "It's supposed to be super-efficient," he explained, showing off the sleek interface on his tablet.

Unfortunately, the app proved a little too efficient. The next morning, Zoey woke to find hundreds of RSVPs from every dog owner in San Francisco.

"Dad!" Zoey wailed. "The app invited the whole city!"

Ray scratched his head. "I don't understand. I only entered a few names..."

As Piper tried to calm a panicking Zoey, Ziggy discreetly accessed the app through the home's Wi-Fi and fixed the glitch, but it was too late to uninvite the extra guests.

The day of the party arrived, and the backyard was transformed into a canine carnival. There were fire hydrant-shaped piñatas, a bone-digging sandbox, and even a "splashzone" with sprinklers controlled by a high-tech panel that Zoey's dad had rigged up.

As the first guests arrived, Zoey pulled Ziggy aside. "Okay, now act surprised!"

"You got it!" Ziggy wagged his tail and let out an enthusiastic "Woof!"

Soon, the backyard was filled with dogs of all shapes and sizes. Buddy the golden retriever bounded in, immediately tangling himself in streamers. Princess the poodle sauntered in, wearing a tiara and looking disdainfully at the "common" decorations.

"Let the games begin!" Zoey announced. "First up, the tail-wagging contest!"

The dogs looked confused. Ziggy, understanding Zoey's intention, began wagging his tail enthusiastically, encouraging the others to join in.

Next came the "best howl" competition, which was

cut short when the neighbors called to complain about the noise. The obstacle course fared no better, with Buddy joyfully destroying half the obstacles and Princess refusing to participate because it might mess up her fur.

Just as things seemed to be falling apart, a sleek van pulled up. Out stepped Mr. Tech with RoverTron 3000, the robot dog from the talent show.

"I heard there was a party," Mr. Tech grinned. "RoverTron 3000 has been upgraded with a new Party Mode!"

Before anyone could stop him, Mr. Tech activated the robot dog. RoverTron's eyes lit up, and suddenly, music began blasting from hidden speakers. The sprinklers went haywire, and tennis balls shot out in all directions.

Chaos erupted. Dogs barked, children squealed, and parents scrambled to regain control. In the midst of it all, Ziggy sprang into action. He discreetly interfaced with RoverTron, modulating the music to a more pleasant volume and redirecting the sprinklers to create a fun splash zone. The tennis ball cannon he repurposed into a fetch-o-matic, much to the delight of the dogs.

As the party got back on track, Zoey watched in amazement. Somehow, every time something went wrong, Ziggy seemed to be there, making it right. It was almost as if he could predict what was going to happen...

Finally, it was time for cake. As everyone sang "Happy Birthday" (with plenty of canine accompaniment), Zoey presented Ziggy with a special gift.

"It's a high-tech collar!" she explained proudly. "It has GPS, health monitoring, and even a translator! Though I guess we don't need that last part, right?" she winked at Ziggy.

Ziggy's eyes widened in surprise and delight.

As the party wound down and guests left with wagging tails and doggy bags, Zoey flopped onto the grass next to Ziggy.

"Well, that was crazy," she giggled. "But fun, right? Happy birthday, Ziggy."

Ziggy nuzzled her hand affectionately. "Thank you, Zoey. It was the best 'birthday' ever."

Zoey smiled, then paused. "You are the best dog and my best friend in the whole world."

Later, as Zoey helped her parents clean up, she couldn't stop thinking about how special Ziggy was.

"He's not like other dogs, is he?" she mused.

"Well," Ray said, picking up stray tennis balls, "he's certainly one of a kind."

That night, as Zoey slept, Ziggy's new collar blinked with an incoming message: "Update complete. New mission parameters incoming." Ziggy's eyes glowed softly in the dark, ready for whatever adventures tomorrow might bring.

8.

The Great Cookie Caper

The heavenly aroma of freshly baked chocolate chip cookies wafted through the house, making Zoey's mouth water as she burst through the front door after school. The scent mingled with the faint hum of the high-tech air purifier Piper had recently installed.

"Mom! Are those your famous cookies?" she called out, dropping her backpack and racing to the kitchen, Ziggy hot on her heels.

Piper smiled, sliding another tray into the sleek, touch-screen oven. "They sure are, sweetie. I'm baking a big batch for the school bake sale tomorrow."

Zoey's eyes widened at the sight of dozens of golden-brown cookies cooling on racks. "Can I have one? Pretty please?"

"Sorry, honey," Piper said, ruffling Zoey's hair. "These are for the sale. But I promise you can have the first one from the next batch."

Zoey pouted but nodded, heading upstairs to do her homework. Ziggy lingered, eyeing the cookies curiously.

"Don't even think about it, mister," Piper warned playfully. Ziggy wagged his tail innocently and trotted after Zoey.

The next morning, a startled cry jolted Zoey awake. She raced downstairs to find her mom staring at the cooling racks in disbelief.

"The cookies! Half of them are gone!" Piper exclaimed.

Zoey gasped. "But how? Did someone break in?"

Piper shook her head. "No signs of a break-in. It's a mystery."

Zoey's eyes lit up. "A mystery? Cool! Ziggy and I can solve it! We'll be like Sherlock Holmes and Dr. Watson!"

Piper couldn't help but smile at her daughter's enthusiasm. "Alright, detective. See what you can find out. I'll bake some more cookies in the meantime."

Zoey grabbed a magnifying glass from her detective kit and began examining the scene, Ziggy at her side. She even donned a deerstalker hat she'd gotten at a tech-themed escape room for her last birthday.

"Look, Ziggy! Crumbs... and tiny paw prints!" she whispered excitedly. "The culprit must be an animal!"

Ziggy sniffed the area, his senses picking up multiple scents. But he kept his discoveries to himself, not wanting to spoil Zoey's fun.

"We need a list of suspects," Zoey declared, grabbing a notebook. "Let's see... Mr. Whiskers, the neighbor's sneaky cat. Buddy, Tommy's clumsy but lovable golden retriever. Ooh, what about Pixie, Mia's tabby cat? Can cats even eat cookies?"

Ziggy nodded, amused by Zoey's reasoning.

"You're right, Zoey! We should add the raccoon family from the park too. They're always getting into trouble!"

Zoey and Ziggy, the dynamic duo, set out to interview their suspects. Mr. Whiskers, more interested in sunbathing than cookies, yawned lazily when questioned. Buddy, though enthusiastic, proved too clumsy for cookie theft, accidentally knocking over a flower pot in his excitement. Pixie reacted grumpily at the mere mention of cookies, clearly showing her dislike for the treats.

As for the raccoons, Zoey and Ziggy spent an amusing hour at the park, trying to communicate with the masked bandits who seemed more interested in Zoey's shoelaces than answering questions.

That night, Zoey decided to set up a stakeout in the kitchen. She positioned herself behind the counter, a flashlight in hand, with Ziggy by her side. She even set up a small security camera she'd borrowed from her dad's smart home kit.

"We'll catch the cookie thief red-handed!" she whispered.

But as the hours ticked by, Zoey's eyelids grew heavy. Soon, she was fast asleep, softly snoring.

The next morning, Zoey was disappointed to find she had fallen asleep on duty. But her disappointment turned to shock when she saw even more cookies were missing – along with other snacks from the pantry!
"There must be more than one thief!" she exclaimed. "But who? And how are they getting in?"

Just then, a soft meow caught their attention. Mr. Whiskers was sitting on the windowsill, looking unusually alert.

"Mr. Whiskers? What are you doing here?" Zoey asked.

The cat meowed again and pawed at the wall. Ziggy's ears perked up, his sensitive hearing picking up a faint scuttling sound.

"Ziggy, what is it? Do you hear something?"

Ziggy replied, "Yes I can hear it", and pawed at the same spot Mr. Whiskers had indicated.

Zoey pressed her ear to the wall. "I hear it too! Tiny feet... in the walls!"

With Piper's permission, Zoey and Ziggy carefully removed a section of baseboard. To their amazement, they found a small door, expertly created from bits of wood and cardboard.

As they watched, the door swung open, and out stepped a mouse. He froze at the sight of Zoey and Ziggy.

The mouse squeaked. Ziggy listened and turned to Zoey. "He says his name is Crumbs and asks that we don't evict him. He's only trying to feed his family." Zoey's eyes widened. "You can understand the mouse?"

Ziggy replied, "Of course I can. All animals can talk to each other?"

After getting over her initial shock, Zoey listened as Ziggy translated Crumbs' explanation of how his mouse family had been struggling to find food. The cookies and pantry raids were acts of desperation. Instead of being angry, Zoey felt sorry for the mice. She thought hard, then smiled as an idea struck her. "I have a plan!" she bent down to talk to the mice.

"We can set up a small 'mouse café' in a quiet corner of the pantry. You can have some of our food, but you have to promise not to take too much or make a mess. Deal?"

Ziggy translated Zoe's idea to Crumbs.
Crumbs' whiskers twitched with joy.

"He says you have a deal and that you're a very kind, young human!"

Zoey ran to ask her mom, "Please, pretty please."

With Piper's amused approval, Zoey set up the mouse café, complete with tiny tables made from bottle caps. She even used her 3D printer to create miniature chairs and plates for the mice. Ziggy was appointed as the watchful "manager" to ensure the mice didn't abuse their privileges.

The cookie mystery was solved, Piper successfully baked a new batch for the bake sale, and peace was restored to the household – with some very happy mice as new neighbors.

That night, as Zoey sighed as she snuggled in bed

with Ziggy. "We make a great team, Ziggy. I wonder if all animals can secretly talk, and we just can't understand them?"

Ziggy nuzzled her hand, thinking to himself how proud he was of her kindness and problem-solving skills.

As Zoey drifted off to sleep, dreaming of talking animals and cookie-loving mice, Ziggy stayed alert, ready for whatever adventure tomorrow might bring.

9.

The Case of the Vanishing Valerie

Zoey's room looked like a tornado had hit it. Clothes were strewn across the floor, books toppled from shelves, and even her mattress was askew. In the middle of this chaos stood Zoey, her face scrunched up in worry.

"Ziggy, I can't find Valerie anywhere!" she cried, turning to her faithful canine companion. "She was right here on my bed last night, and now she's gone!" Valerie wasn't just any doll. She was a high-tech interactive toy that Uncle Neo had given her on her last birthday. With her ability to talk, and play games, Valerie had quickly become Zoey's favorite possession. The doll's sleek design, with her color-changing hair and interactive touch screen on her dress, made her the envy of all of Zoey's friends.

Ziggy's ears perked up, already thinking of possible scenarios.

"I think I saw her on your bed last night," said Ziggy.

He began sniffing around the room, trying to pick up a scent trail.

"Good idea, Ziggy!" Zoey exclaimed. "You can smell where she went!"

As they searched, Zoey rambled nervously. "Maybe she fell behind the bed? Or got buried under my stuffed animals? Oh, what if someone stole her?"

As Zoey and Ziggy were about to search, they ran into Zoey's parents in the hallway.

"Mom! Dad! Have you seen Valerie?" Zoey asked frantically.

Her parents exchanged a worried glance. "Oh no," her mom said. "We meant to tell you this morning, but we were in such a rush..."

"Tell me what?" Zoey asked, her brow furrowing. Her dad sighed. "We found Valerie in the kitchen sink early this morning. She seemed to be malfunctioning – trying to 'swim' or something. There must be a glitch in her programming."

"We had to get her out and dry her off," her mom added. "But then we got caught up in getting ready for work, and we... well, we forgot where we put her."

"She's somewhere around," her dad assured her. "We just can't remember exactly where. I'm sure you'll find her, sweetheart."

With that, her parents hurried off to work, leaving Zoey and Ziggy with this new information.

"Did you hear that, Ziggy?" Zoey said. "Valerie's got a glitch, and she's somewhere in the house. We've got to find her!"

In the living room, they met Mr. Whiskers, the neighbor's cat who often snuck in through the pet door. He was lounging on the windowsill, looking suspiciously smug.

"Mr. Whiskers, have you seen Valerie?" Zoey asked, not really expecting an answer.

To her surprise, the cat meowed and flicked his tail towards the backyard, as if pointing.

"Did... did he just answer me?" Zoey wondered aloud, glancing at Ziggy.

Ziggy didn't answer.

As they headed to the backyard, Zoey heard a familiar voice. "Hey, Zoey! Whatcha doing?"

It was Tommy, watching Buddy dig enthusiastic holes in their yard.

"I've lost Valerie," Zoey explained. "Have you seen her?"

Tommy shook his head, but Buddy's ears perked up at the word "lost." With a joyful bark, he bounded over the fence, ready to join the search.

"Buddy, no!" Tommy called, but it was too late. The overjoyed dog was already racing around Zoey's yard, sniffing everything in sight and leaving a trail of muddy pawprints.

"Some help you are," Zoey giggled, as Buddy's "search" resulted in knocking over a flowerpot and tangling himself in the garden hose.

Just then, Mia appeared, her tabby cat Pixie trotting beside her. "I heard you lost something," she said. "Maybe Pixie can help! She has extraordinary senses that can detect electronic signals."

Zoey's eyes lit up. "Valerie is full of electronics! That's perfect!"

Pixie began scanning the area, meowing softly. Suddenly, she took off down the street, with the whole gang in pursuit.

Their wild chase led them through the neighborhood, following various electronic signals. They found lost phones, forgotten tablets, and even an old radio in Mr. Johnson's garage, but no Valerie.

The search eventually took them to the park, near the raccoons' favorite tree.
"Oh no," Zoey groaned. "Please don't tell me the raccoons took Valerie!"

They approached cautiously, finding the raccoon family playing with an assortment of shiny objects – keys, coins, even a sparkly bracelet. But there was no sign of Valerie.

They trudged home, disappointed.

Suddenly, Ziggy stopped. "I've got an idea," he said.. He raced to the laundry room.

"What is it, Ziggy?" Zoey asked, following him. "Did you find her?"

Ziggy jumped on top of the washing machine. Zoey looked confused, but opened the door — and gasped.

There, nestled among the dirty clothes, was Valerie!

"Valerie!" Zoey cried, scooping up the doll. "But how did you get in here?"

Just then, Zoey's parents walked in, looking both relieved and a bit sheepish.

Zoey's dad said, running a hand through his hair. "We put her in the laundry basket to dry out and forgot to tell you. We're so sorry, honey."

Zoey hugged Valerie tight, then reached down to pat Ziggy. "You're amazing, Ziggy! How did you know to look in the laundry room?"

Ziggy wagged his tail, and didn't say a thing..

That night, as Zoey slept peacefully with both Valerie and Ziggy by her side, Ziggy kept one eye open, watching the doll carefully.

10.

Camping Trip Chaos

The SUV bounced along the bumpy dirt road, loaded to the brim with camping gear. Zoey's face was pressed against the window, her eyes wide with excitement as she took in the towering trees and glimpses of wildlife.

"Look, Ziggy!" she exclaimed, pointing at a deer darting between the trees. "Isn't this amazing?"

"It certainly is," Ziggy replied, his tail wagging. "I can't wait to explore!"

As they pulled into the campsite, Ray let out a low whistle. "Well, gang, welcome to our home for the next three days!"

Piper smiled as she stretched her legs. "Alright, let's get our camp set up before it gets dark."

The family struggled to set up the campsite. Ray, trying to put up the tent, only managed to tangle himself up in the canvas. Piper's attempts to start a fire resulted in more smoke than flame.

"Zoey," Ziggy whispered, "maybe we should help your dad with the tent. The pole he needs is right behind him."

Zoey giggled and handed her dad the correct pole. "Here, Dad! Is this what you need?"

Ray looked surprised. "Thanks, sweetie! How did you know?"

Zoey just shrugged, sharing a secret smile with Ziggy.

Once camp was set up, Piper suggested a short nature walk before dinner. As they hiked along the trail,

Ziggy's sensors were on high alert, picking up on wildlife that the humans couldn't see or hear.

"Zoey," Ziggy said quietly, "there's a fox in those bushes to your right. Watch closely."

Seconds later, a beautiful fox emerged, regarding them curiously before disappearing back into the underbrush.

"Wow, Ziggy!" Zoey exclaimed. "How did you know it was there?"

"I could smell it," Ziggy replied.

As they continued their walk, Ziggy helped spot a family of deer, a rare woodpecker, and even a well-camouflaged owl. Each time, Zoey's amazement at Ziggy's abilities grew.

On their way back to the campsite, Zoey was so busy chatting with Ziggy that she didn't notice when they took a wrong turn at a fork in the trail. It wasn't until the path started to look unfamiliar that she realized they were lost.

"Mom? Dad?" Zoey called out, trying to keep the panic out of her voice. But there was no response.

"Don't worry, Zoey," Ziggy said reassuringly. "I can get us back to the campsite. Just follow me."

"You know the way?" Zoey asked, hope creeping into her voice.

"Trust me," Ziggy replied, leading her confidently down a path.

As they walked, they had several unexpected encounters. A curious squirrel chattered at them from a low branch.

"He's asking if we have any nuts," Ziggy translated. Zoey giggled. "Really? That's so cool! Too bad we don't have any to share."

Their journey took an exciting turn when they stumbled upon a bear's den. Zoey froze in terror, but Ziggy quickly spoke up.

"Don't panic, Zoey," he said calmly. "We need to back away slowly. Don't run or make any sudden movements."

Zoey nodded, trusting Ziggy. "Okay, what else should we do?"

"Make some calm, non-threatening noises as we leave. It'll let the bear know we're not trying to sneak up on it."

Following Ziggy's instructions, they safely retreated from the area. Once they were a safe distance away, Zoey hugged Ziggy tightly. "You saved us, Ziggy! How did you know what to do?"

Ziggy wagged his tail. "Let's just say I've done my research on forest safety."

Finally, they made it back to the campsite, where Piper and Ray were just about to organize a search party. There were hugs all around, with Ziggy receiving extra pats and a special treat for bringing Zoey home safely.

That night, as they sat around the campfire roasting marshmallows, Zoey couldn't stop talking about their adventure.

"And then Ziggy spotted an owl that was so well hidden, I couldn't see it even when he pointed it out! And he knew exactly what to do when we saw the bear's den. He's like... a super wilderness dog or something!"

Ray chuckled. "Well, I'm just glad you're both safe. Ziggy certainly earned his kibble today!"

As Zoey snuggled into her sleeping bag that night with Ziggy curled up next to her, she whispered, "Ziggy, you're the best dog ever. I'm so glad you can talk to me."

"I'm glad too, Zoey," Ziggy replied softly. "Now get some sleep. We've got more adventures waiting for us tomorrow."

In the middle of the night, a band of raccoons attempted to raid their food supply. Ziggy woke up and whispered to Zoey, "We've got some midnight visitors. Want to help me chase them away?"

Ziggy led Zoey on a silent chase around the campsite herding the raccoons away without waking her parents.

As dawn broke and the family began to pack up their gear, the ranger's radio crackled to life with news that a child had gone missing in the woods. Without hesitation, Zoey volunteered herself and Ziggy to help with the search.

"Please, Mom, Dad," she begged. "Ziggy's amazing at finding things in the woods. We can help!"

Reluctantly, her parents agreed, and soon Ziggy was leading the search party through the forest. He whispered clues to Zoey, who then "spotted" the signs for the adults – a scrap of fabric here, a faint footprint there.

Finally, they found the lost child, a young boy who had wandered away from his campsite. As the rangers praised Ziggy's "incredible nose," Zoey hugged her furry friend tightly.

"You're a hero, Ziggy!" she whispered.

"We're a team," Ziggy replied warmly. "I couldn't have done it without you."

As they drove home later that day, Zoey couldn't stop recounting their adventures. Ziggy, curled up in the backseat, listened contentedly.

11.

The Truth Unleashed

$\mathcal{T}$he park buzzed with the usual weekend activity — kids laughing, dogs barking, and parents chatting. The air was filled with the faint hum of drones capturing aerial footage for a local news story. Zoey and Ziggy were in their favorite spot near the pond, enjoying a game of fetch.

"Okay, Ziggy," Zoey grinned, waving a tennis ball. "Let's see if you can get this one!"

She threw the ball with all her might, sending it soaring over the pond. Ziggy watched its arc, sprinted around the pond at a great speed, leapt into the air, and caught the ball just before it hit the water.

Zoey's jaw dropped. "Ziggy? How did you...?"
Before Ziggy could respond, a piercing scream cut through the air. A toddler had wandered onto the thin ice covering part of the pond, and it was beginning to crack.

Without thinking, Ziggy sprang into action. His eyes glowed as he activated his thermal imaging, identifying the safest path across the ice. In a blur of motion, he dashed across the pond, scooped up the child in his mouth, and deposited her safely on the shore - all in under ten seconds.

The park erupted in cheers, but Zoey stood stock-still, her face pale. She had seen Ziggy's eyes glow. She had seen him move faster than any dog could. And now, as Ziggy turned to her, she heard him speak - but out loud for everyone to hear.

"It's okay," Ziggy was saying to the crying toddler. "You're safe now."

The girl's mother rushed over, scooping up her child and thanking Ziggy profusely. But Ziggy's eyes were locked on Zoey, who was backing away slowly, shaking her head in disbelief.

"Zoey," Ziggy said softly, approaching her. "I can explain."

"Stay away from me!" Zoey cried, turning and running towards home.

Ziggy followed at a distance; his heart heavy. When they reached Zoey's house, she ran straight to her room and slammed the door. Ziggy sat outside, waiting.

Hours passed. Finally, the door creaked open. Zoey's eyes were red from crying.

"Come in," she said quietly.

Ziggy entered cautiously. Zoey sat on her bed, hugging her knees.

"What are you?" she asked, her voice barely a whisper.

Ziggy took a deep breath. "I'm a cyborg. I have biological parts combined with AI - Artificial Intelligence, a robot skeleton, and a special brain. I was created to be a companion and protector."

Zoey's eyes widened. "So... you're part robot?"

"In a way, yes," Ziggy replied. "I look and feel like a dog, but my mind and some of my body are different. More advanced."

Zoey was quiet for a long moment. "Why didn't you tell me?"

"I was afraid," Ziggy admitted. "Afraid you wouldn't understand, that you'd see me differently. I never meant to deceive you, Zoey. Everything we've shared—our friendship, our adventures - it's all been real."

Zoey's eyes filled with tears. "But how can I know that? How can I trust anything now?"

Ziggy's ears drooped. "Because despite being an AI, I've learned what it means to love, to care, to be a friend. And it's all because of you, Zoey. You're my best friend, and that's the truest thing I know."

Zoey looked at him, really looked at him. She saw the same eyes that had watched over her, the same fur she had hugged when she was sad, the same Ziggy who had been by her side through everything.

Slowly, she reached out and placed her hand on Ziggy's head. "You're still my Ziggy, aren't you?"

Ziggy's tail wagged hopefully. "Always, Zoey. Always."
Zoey threw her arms around him, burying her face in his fur. "I'm sorry I ran away. I was just so shocked and scared."

"I understand," Ziggy said, nuzzling her. "I'm sorry I kept this from you for so long."

Zoey pulled back, wiping her eyes. A small smile played on her lips. "So... what else can you do?"

Ziggy's eyes twinkled. "Well, how about we start with how I can help you ace that science project?"

Sneak peek at Ziggy and Zoey Book –2

Ziggy and Zoey's Paw-some Adventures
The Science Fair Sensation

1.

Project Impossible

Zoey burst into her room, her backpack swinging wildly as she flung it onto her bed. "Ziggy! Ziggy! You won't believe what Mrs. Maple announced today!"

Ziggy, who had been lounging on his cushion, perked up his ears. Since Zoey had discovered his true nature as an AI, their conversations had become much more open and exciting. "What is it, Zoey? Did they finally agree to serve pizza every day in the cafeteria?"

Zoey giggled, shaking her head. "No, silly! Even better. We're having a science fair next month!"

Ziggy's tail began to wag. "A science fair? That does sound exciting. I assume you want to enter?"

"Of course!" Zoey exclaimed, flopping down next to Ziggy. "And now that I know about your super-smart AI mind, we can create something really amazing together!"

Ziggy's eyes twinkled with amusement. "Just remember, I'm supposed to be a regular dog to everyone else. We can't have me giving a lecture on quantum physics."

Zoey rolled her eyes. "I know, I know. But you can still help me come up with ideas, right?"

"Absolutely," Ziggy replied. "What kind of project did you have in mind?"

Zoey's face scrunched up in thought. "Well, I want it to be something really cool. Not just a baking soda volcano or a potato battery."

"Those are classics for a reason," Ziggy chuckled. "But I agree, we can aim higher. What if we combined different kinds of science? We could create something that's not only impressive but also helpful."

Zoey's eyes lit up. "Ooh, like an eco-friendly, AI-powered invention?"

"Now you're thinking!" Ziggy said enthusiastically. "What kind of problem would you like to solve?"

For the next hour, Zoey and Ziggy bounced ideas back and forth. They considered everything from a solar-powered robot that could clean up litter to a device that could translate animal sounds. Finally, they settled on a project: a smart garden system that could optimize plant growth while conserving water and energy.

"This is perfect!" Zoey exclaimed. "We can use recycled materials for the structure, and you can help me do coding."

Ziggy nodded approvingly. "It's a great choice. It combines environmental science, computer programming, and biology. Plus, it's something that could really make a difference."

Over the next few days, Zoey threw herself into research. She pored over books about plant biology and water conservation, while Ziggy helped explain some of the more complex concepts in terms she could understand.

"So, if we use sensors to monitor the soil moisture," Zoey mused, sketching out a design, "can we make sure each plant gets exactly the right amount of water?"

"Exactly," Ziggy confirmed. "And we can add light sensors too, to adjust the LED grow lights for the best photosynthesis."

As they worked on their blueprint, Zoey couldn't help but marvel at how much easier it was now that she knew about Ziggy's true nature.

With their plan in place, they began gathering materials. Zoey collected empty plastic bottles, old pipes, and bits of wire from around the house.

Meanwhile, Zoey ordered some specialized components online, with her mom.

The real fun began when they started building their prototype. Zoey's bedroom transformed into a makeshift laboratory, with tools and parts scattered everywhere. Her parents peeked in occasionally, smiling at her enthusiasm but wisely choosing not to ask too many questions about the complex-looking mechanism taking shape.

"Hand me that screwdriver, Ziggy," Zoey said, her tongue sticking out slightly as she concentrated on connecting two parts.

Ziggy obliged, using his mouth to carefully pass her the tool.

As they worked, they encountered several challenges. The water pump wasn't powerful enough, the first batch of sensors wasn't waterproof, and their initial attempts at codingI resulted in some hilarious malfunctions.

"Zoey," Ziggy said one afternoon, staring at their creation, "I don't think petunias are supposed to get that much water."

Zoey looked up from her tablet to see their test plant practically drowning. "Oops! I think I put a decimal point in the wrong place in the code."

They laughed together as they rushed to save the waterlogged flower, Ziggy secretly using some of his advanced capabilities to quickly debug the program while Zoey wasn't looking.

As the science fair approached, their smart garden system began to take shape. It was a marvel of recycled materials and cutting-edge technology, with plants already beginning to thrive under its care.

The night before the fair, Zoey practiced her presentation one last time. Ziggy listened attentively, offering encouragement and gentle suggestions for improvement.

"You've got this, Zoey," he said warmly as she finished. "Your project is amazing, and more importantly, you understand every part of it. You should be very proud."

Zoey beamed, kneeling down to hug her furry friend. "I couldn't have done it without you, Ziggy. Thank you for everything."

As they prepared for bed, both girl and dog were buzzing with excitement for the next day. Their invention was safely packed away, ready to be transported to the school gymnasium in the morning.

Just as Zoey was drifting off to sleep, a loud crash of thunder shook the house. Her eyes flew open to see rain lashing against her window.

"Oh no!" she gasped, sitting up in bed. "Ziggy, what if the rain damages our project on the way to school tomorrow?"

Ziggy's mind raced, calculating possibilities. "Don't worry, Zoey. We'll figure something out. After all, we're a team, remember?"

Zoey nodded as another flash of lightning illuminated the room. Come rain or shine, she and Ziggy were ready to face whatever challenges the science fair might bring. Their greatest adventure yet was about to begin.

About the Author

Pragya Tomar is a passionate children's author and the founder of PenMagicBooks Publishing. She has a love of storytelling, imbuing her stories with a magical touch and fantastical adventures that quickly make them favorites of kids of all ages. She believes that stories are a wonderful way of inspiring kids and introducing them to reading at a young age, and she hopes that her books will touch their hearts and make their childhoods that little bit more special.

Pragya has worked in the Animation Industry as a Visual FX Artist. There she's brought her magic touch to critically-acclaimed feature films and shows including Disney's Bolt, A Christmas Carol, Cloudy With a Chance of Meatballs, Star Wars, Transformers 3, Kungfu Panda, Nickelodeon's TV show WallyKazam and Shimmer and Shine.

For more information on her and the whole team at PenMagicBooks, visit: www.penmagicbooks.com @Insta handle author_pragyatomar

Made in the USA
Las Vegas, NV
16 November 2024

11519718R10066